Ukraine Refugees

Echoes of War

Francois

Thanks for the idea that we would make great futurologists

Chris

Ukraine Refugees

Echoes of War

Aaron Aalborg

Copyright Page

This novel is a work of fiction. Names, characters, and incidents either are the product of the author's imagination or used fictitiously and any resemblance to actual persons, living or dead, businesses, locations or events is entirely coincidental.

Copyright © 2022 by Chris J. Clarke.
All rights reserved. Neither this book or parts thereof may be reproduced in any form without permission.

ISBN-13: 978-0-9996371-2-8

First Edition March 2022

Editing, cover design, and formatting
By Sabertooth Books

Published by Penman House Publishing

PENMAN HOUSE
PUBLISHING

Dedication

To all those who care about the suffering of refugees and victims of wars;

especially to those who provide action as well as words.

All profits from the sale of this book will be donated to non-religious charities helping refugees. Those paying their leaders excessively will be excluded.

Acknowledgements

Thanks are due to Bob Brashears, the moderator of the Costa Rica Writers Group, for encouragement and editing. To Calvin Cahail, who did a superb and rapid job of producing the intentionally disturbing cover design, formatting and more.

Introduction

The horrible videos of death and mutilation, the bereavements and the gut-wrenching distress of the survivors cut into our souls. No writing can surpass these nightmare scenes.

This book is based on true events. Yet partly set in the unknowable future, it is therefore a novel. Any resemblance to real individuals is entirely coincidental. All characters are heavily disguised.

From a period that began in the Soviet era, your author, Aaron Aalborg, visited, worked, and had businesses in most of the countries deeply involved in the geopolitics of the Ukrainian war, including in Kyiv.[1] The hatreds and memories of recent and older repressions, ethnic cleansing, and war crimes, run deep in almost all Ukrainians. The same applies to Poles, Slovaks, Romanians, Hungarians and others.

---

[1] Until this war, westernized spelling and pronunciation were used for locations in the Ukraine and are not used anymore; as the media has adopted and popularized Ukrainian pronunciation and spelling, these are used in this novel.

Ukraine Refugees

This explains the special empathy these nationalities have with the plight of these refugees.

For a time, it seemed that economic and social progress might be made in Ukraine. Then it was shattered.

Many millions of Ukrainians will settle in their host countries or return to rebuild their homeland. The dramatic future events foretold in this book will apply to just a small percentage. To a degree, some of the issues and difficulties will apply to all. This should not stop the charitable actions of the many who have stepped forward. If it causes deeper thought over knee jerk reactions, that is surely a good thing.

***

My two brothers and their wives were among the well over 150,000 UK householders seeking to offer homes and support to some of the dispossessed and traumatized Ukrainians. The UK has not offered sufficient entry permits for all of them to be satisfied.[2]

---

[2] The total numbers of Ukrainians fleeing their homes is reported as 4 million.

Most braved death, hardship, and agony to escape. Years later, many will still have heart-wrenching anxiety for dead or missing family members. Some will always fear further war.

Earnest family discussions about offering safe havens to refugees gave me realistic insights into the issues involved. Experiences from hosts' generosity might form the basis for a second book.

The writer bows to the anger of the estimated forty million refugees from the many other countries that did and still do suffer from war, famine, or political oppression. Many are from Africa, the Middle East, the Far East, and Latin America. Millions are stuck or dying in transit. Others starve in squalid camps. Some are left in cheap accommodations in destination countries for years, without adequate support. Photographs and videos are horrific. From these other countries they are even worse. The dull, dying eyes of starving babies looking out from emaciated skulls and skeletal bodies are unbearable.

Quite rightly, other refugees ask, "What about us?"

At least part of the answer lies in the shared recent history, proximity, and cultural ties that the Ukraine has with other European countries. The plight of other refugees must not be ignored.

Ukraine Refugees

The shocking experiences of Ukrainian refugees apply to these others. Theirs are often much worse, with much less hope of aid.

1

The Straw that Broke the Camel's Back

Jack and Anne were young retirees and empty nesters. They argued a lot.

Both were married at the time, when she had been his secretary, and was ten years younger. Her first husband had started hitting her early in the marriage. She divorced, garnering significant wealth, as he was the scion of a newspaper family.

Jack was rich, handsome, and silver-tongued. Of course, his wife did not understand him. His divorce followed the discovery of his affair with Anne.

Jack and Anne's grown children lived in California and Wisconsin with their own kids. They had busy lives. Visits to the large colonial style family home in Connecticut were disappointingly and increasingly rare. They had horrible memories of the screaming parental rows, fights and separations they experienced growing up.

***

Ukraine Refugees

"Why don't we downsize?" proposed Jack. He had raised the issue before, saying they could even move to be near his favorite daughter in California.

Anne countered, "Things might change. The children could even find work nearer to here. Stamford and New York offer huge opportunities and are easily commutable."

Both were aware that their offspring might have good reasons for wanting to stay away. Since marrying Anne, Jack had had a few affairs with co-workers at his investment bank. Anne had a month-long affair with a neighbor's husband while Jack was on business trips, or on his supposed golf weekends.

When she discovered his adultery, there had been blazing anger. Things were thrown. Drunkenness and yelled threats of divorce sent the children screaming to hide under their beds.

It took many sessions of marriage and family counselling, child psychologists and time for everyone to paper over the cracks. The psychological damage still loomed beneath the surface.

Anne often told herself, *Just one more thing and that's it. Finished!*

***

The Russian invasion of Ukraine caused additional stress. Night after night, Anne and Jack had watched the violence escalate on the news channels. Jack tended to rant. "The US pretty well invited an invasion by promising only sanctions rather than direct military intervention. We needed to be firm. JFK knew how to face down the Russians."

Bored by his nightly diatribes, Anne pointed out the risks of a third world war. "There would be no safe place, especially here, so close to the financial capital of the world. Putin's crazy enough to do it."

The media showed hospitals full of wounded, homes blown apart, and mutilated children dying in the street. Many evenings they both wept. Anne and Jack had red eyes and the heaving chests of helpless sympathy. Like children, they sought solace in hugs. What else could they do?

***

Months passed. Hordes of hungry, deeply damaged people streamed away from death and destruction into Poland, Slovakia, and Romania. Some even fled eastward into Turkey, Russia, Belarus, and Moldova. Many of those fleeing east did so because they feared reprisals from western Ukrainians. Western Ukrainians were lured east by false promises of protection, work, and better conditions.

The peoples of Europe mostly wanted to help. How could anyone turn their backs on the desperate, especially when many had memories of their own recent history at the hands of Hitler, Stalin, and their successors?

Ukraine Refugees

***

Some politicians, particularly in the US and UK, did not want the expense and problems of further waves of immigration. Eventually, they caved to popular pressure. Many bureaucratic obstacles remained. To various degrees, they opened their gates.

All the while, the tear-jerking videos continued.

***

Anne and Jack took to switching channels to hide from the ever more distressing news. One night every news show had the same stories. They seemed to be competing for the bloodiest pictures.

Anne blurted out, "We have a large house. We could offer a home for a while."

She was surprised that Jack agreed. "Let's look into it." He meant it too.

Over the next days, Jack went into his analytical, investment banker's mode. Anne's emotions and instincts did not change. He drew up columns "for" and "against." He listed the issues that might arise. *We are more fortunate than most. Financially we could easily handle it.*

Jack began to envisage obstacles. They worried him. He began to lose sleep, with night sweats and ever more concerns. His thoughts ran on and on. *Helping the refugees would become a full-time job. English lessons, finding schools, welfare, and work, chauffeuring them to appointments, driving lessons and more would be huge commitments. They would need an additional car or we'd have to shell out for taxi fares.*

I like my golf and fishing trips. Opportunities for my bit of fun on the side would dry up.

Anne would feel obliged to get them private medical care to short circuit the US's bureaucratic and impoverished health system. Just because we're comfortably off, does not mean I want to spend too much on strangers. The Ukrainians will soon befriend compatriots who already live nearby. This would certainly help with support and integration. On the other hand, their friends would soon come to our house. There would be less or no time for our friends.

He voiced some of his concerns. "What if they want to join anti-Russian protests and groups? They'll be angry as hell. I would be. They could get mixed up in illegal activities and seek to bring over more family members."

Jack had done business in post-Soviet Russia. He was surprised at the level of support for Putin back then among the bank's senior team in both St. Petersburg and Moscow. Current Russian contacts told him that this continued, despite US claims that Putin was teetering. This was just not reported in the US media. He well knew that propaganda ruled in times of international tension. It was impossible to know the truth.

His concerns mounted. *Some of our neighbors, our housekeepers, and gardeners might resent refugees. The latest wave of immigrants is always seen as a threat to the livelihood of previous groups.*

***

The Russian mafia has been in the US for many years. Come to think of it, that enormous estate near ours is reputedly owned by one of them. The massive gates look as though they were brought from a European fortress. Two no-neck, pasty-faced heavies with bulgy jackets scrutinize all cars passing by.

Jack remembered that, in Russia, only the village idiot smiles at strangers. Hence the guards had steely stares. Sometimes, three dark-colored Cadillac Escalades with blacked out windows emerged in convoy. They seemed heavy on their suspensions. *Maybe it's armor plate?*

Russian gangsters are as ruthless as Putin – maybe worse. No wonder we never invite them to "get to know the neighbors" barbeques. What if the Ukrainians we get are alcoholics? What if Anne takes a fancy to a handsome young immigrant? Nothing will be as before. They'll have different food, waking hours, and music. On balance, it's likely that every Ukrainian will experience difficulties and stress. Picking those that are suitable is a key step.

***

Anne developed her own dreams about new members of her household. She shared them with Jack. "It would be nice to have children around here again."

"You must be kidding! We agreed, 'No more,' before I had that vasectomy. Besides, that would involve schools, noise, and probably bullying by other kids. They pick on anyone who's different."

"It was you who insisted on the snip. I would have liked more."

"Have you thought it might nix any chances of our kids being more friendly and visiting?"

***

Anne started to develop her own worries. She looked up Ukrainian food on the internet.
Borscht sounds quite nice, but garlic fritters are out. Jack freaks out if he smells garlic in the house. That Sal, pork fat on Rye bread sounds Yuk! These other

things look nasty too. Imagine the mess in the kitchen.

What if Jack were to run off with a pretty, younger Ukrainian? He told me I'm getting a "little matronly," only a couple of weeks back. She clicked on a few websites. *These pictures show that many are blond and blue-eyed. Just his type. Ha! The old goat is not that particular. Any type will do after a few drinks. That's it then! No females younger than me – and not attractive either.*

***

They had started the application process. The social worker on the vetting team quickly surfaced the differences of opinion. She added various questions to the forms. Her case team members agreed with her concerns. Jack and Anne were classed as "unsuitable."

The blazing rows began. Anne visited a divorce lawyer and that was that.

***

Jack took an apartment in Stamford. He poured himself a stiff thirty-year-old Macallan scotch, then switched on his Mac Book. After a few keystrokes, he found Ukrainia_love.com. He drooled over the seemingly endless parade of keen and gorgeous lovelies. *These are the refugees for me. Maybe I could try a few out?*

2

The Defectors' Tale

In October 2021, 22-year-old Mládshiy Leytenánt Pavel Sidarov was enjoying a few days home leave from his tank regiment.

He and his wife, Alina, had a small apartment on the 5th floor of a Soviet era apartment block. There were no elevators, so it was a difficult walk up for any old or infirm residents. Alina had struggled during her recent pregnancy.

Pavel was holding his new-born son, Konstantin, a little awkwardly. The boy was swaddled in many layers of blankets against the cold drafts knifing through the window frames into the warm fug of the room. Pavel had arrived only the day before. He was looking forward to being with his wife and some home cooking. There was a banging on the door. It was Granny Inessa, from another apartment.

"Hurry Pavel. There's a call from your boss. It sounds important."

He raised his eyes to the ceiling, thrust the baby into his wife's clasp and hurried to the phone at the other end of the corridor. "Yes, Mládshiy Leytenánt Sidarov here."

He stood to attention as the major spoke. "Yes, Mayór. I understand. Right, Sir. I'll pack and leave straight away."

***

His disappointment at his curtailed leave was partly compensated by his joy at the prospect of a huge exercise on the Ukraine border. Like many young men, his hormones and personality had driven him to join up, seeking action and comradeship. He put on his smart junior lieutenant's uniform. Then, with the briefest goodbyes, he rushed down to a waiting transport. It contained three others, grim faced and silent. He noted their patches. One was in the artillery; the lanky guy next to him was a sergeant in a recon unit. The last man wore no patches, he looked especially tough. *He must be Spetsnaz, Special Forces.*

The sergeant passed a two-liter bottle of vodka round in the bouncing truck. They finished it before they reached the train station, without showing any obvious effects. Most Russians drank vodka like water. The army was no exception. That was one reason why national life expectancy was so low.

***

Ukraine Refugees

At the Ukraine border, his tank crew awaited him. He loved his T-72. With a crew of three, it was lighter and faster than its NATO counterparts. When pushed, it could fly over obstacles at 47kpm (30 miles per hour). The gun featured auto-loading and fired many rounds a minute. Like most of his men, he itched to test it in combat. Blowing things apart was a blast in more ways than one.

The exercises progressed. His crew was at peak efficiency and fitness. *What next?*

***

They received the order to invade Ukraine on February 23, 2022. Their start line was in Donbas, a Russian-speaking region already controlled by rebels supporting Russia. The tankers first objective was Mariupol, then ever deeper into Ukraine. *It'll be easy.*

They crashed through the border. The mixed line of tanks, BTR-wheeled, and BMP-tracked, personnel carriers and trucks drove fast down the main road. The roar and smoke from a hundred diesel engines filled the air.

Things went wrong on the outskirts of Mariupol,

***

Pavel sat in the open hatch of his tank. It was the number six vehicle in the convoy. The heavy machine gun was swung out of the way, to give him a clear view of the road ahead.

He did not hear the shot over the roar of the engine, but he saw the commander of the BPM in front of him slump over its turret.

Yelling into his mic, "Sniper!" he dropped into the turret, clanging down the hatch. Looking through the all-round optics, he saw that both the BPM and another vehicle ahead took hits from above. The initial blinding flashes were followed by bigger explosions.

"Get us off the road! They have Javelins."[3] He swung the turret with its massive gun, looking for likely sniper sites.

The obvious place was a large residential block. It looked like his home, but the adrenaline was pumping. "Four rounds, rapid fire, high explosive. Fourth and fifth floors. Fire!"

---

[3]The Javelin is a highly portable, US made anti-tank rocket. It uses infrared guidance. Once locked on it can hit a moving target, whilst the crew gets away from the launch site. Its best shot is to strike from above. It defeats the reactive armor of Russian tanks by using a double warhead. The explosive sets off the reactive armor's counter-explosion; the main warhead penetrates the armor plate.

The entire side of the building collapsed. The T-72 behind him was hit as it slewed off the road. Seconds

later his track hit a mine. It jolted the crew upwards, hard. His skull was saved from impact with the turret armor by his helmet.

"Bail out, fast!" He and the gunner dragged the unconscious driver out of the disabled vehicle. Then there was a bang! Everything went blank.

***

Pavel awoke in a Ukrainian field hospital. His head was swimming. He had drips into both arms. *I can't feel my left arm at all.* The lights were dazzling. He noticed a heavily armed guard by the door, as he drifted in and out of consciousness.

A Russian officer accompanied a white-coated doctor into the room. The officer smiled, speaking Russian. Pavel understood, as most Ukrainians can. Years of oppression had seen to that. "You see. We are taking good care of you. We know you were ordered to invade against your will."

Pavel remained silent. He was trained to do that.

In the next 24 hours things moved fast. An orderly shared the news that they wanted him to hear. "Your armored column has been liquidated. Unfortunately, your men fired on civilian buildings. Many women and children were killed and wounded.

"Our government is going to charge all Russian officers with war crimes. You'll probably be shot. Our troops in charge of this area lost relatives – dead, injured and missing in Mariupol. You'll be glad when they finally shoot you."

***

Two officers entered the ward along with a soldier carrying a small movie camera. One was the one from before. The second was a tough-looking man, stern-faced and heavily muscled. His nose had been broken at some point. The close-cropped stubble emphasised his bull neck.

The hard man barked out. "Did you knowingly target civilian buildings?"

"Of course not! My tank never fired at civilians."

"Were you ordered to capture Mariupol regardless of opposition?"

"Yes. We had tight deadlines."

The benign officer smiled. "If you were ordered to do things you did not want to do, you will be released when all this is over."

***

Ukraine Refugees

So, Junior Lieutenant Pavel appeared on news programs around the world, except in Russia. Back home, FSB officers smashed down his apartment door. Baby Konstantin was roughly torn from screaming Alina's arms. She tried to cling to him, receiving a brutal blow to her face from a pistol. She was dragged away in hysterics.

***

Two years after the peace treaty was signed, Pavel was living in a small, terraced house in Leeds, in England. His new name was Vladislav Ivanov. He worked as a gardener for the municipality.

His captors realized that he was of little use as an intelligence source. They had higher profile defectors for publicity purposes. On the other hand, if he were to return to Russia, a show trial would reflect badly on NATO and western democracy. They kept him without a passport.

His life was miserable. His English was improving, but unlike Ukrainian refugees, he had to stay away from all Russians, and especially from potentially vengeful Ukrainians. The unknown fate of his wife and son kept him awake at night. Most of his wages went on Vodka.

A year later an envelope dropped through the flap of the letter box in his door.

***

Tearing it open, he gripped a photograph in both his shaking hands. Collapsing into a chair, he wept to see Alina. She looked years older. She was haggard, with grey hair, bundled up against the cold. The bleak landscape was covered in snow. *Siberia?*

He leafed through the other contents of the package. A fierce looking nurse was holding an infant. *Konstantin?*

There was an unsigned letter, with no letterhead.

> *Pavel,*
>
> *We can ensure that you are safely returned to the Russian Federation.*
>
> *You will face a military court.*
>
> *You will say that you were drugged and tortured by the CIA to make the video.*
>
> *Then, after a minimal time in prison, you will be reunited with your family, given a new identity, and relocated in a different city.*
>
> *We will contact you.*

Breathing hard he examined the contents again. *What to do?*

***

Should I contact the British authorities, or maybe the Americans? The SVR obviously knows my whereabouts. I'll be watched. If I try to seek help, they'll kill me. I would never see my wife or boy again.

He nervously looked out of the window. The parked cars in the street seemed empty. *Nothing! If I go along with this, I risk my life.*

***

The next three weeks were a nightmare. He hardly slept, drinking even more than usual. Not knowing what will happen next is the worst thing. He started to suspect the neighbors. Apart from a morning, "Hey up," or "Ow do," he did not know them. At work, he watched the others he met. *It's driving me crazy.*

Then a further letter came through the flap, whilst he was asleep. It gave a location in the suburb of Morely. It told him to be there at 10 a.m. two days hence. He worried even more, hardly sleeping.

***

He took three buses, scrutinizing the other passengers. He arrived at the meeting place at 7 a.m. to check the place out. He looked around. There was a derelict warehouse and an abandoned parking lot. He saw only a few people and cars, all in the far distance.

At 11 a.m., he began to fret *Am I in the wrong place?* Then a grey Range Rover with dark windows slowly drove up, trailing dust. It stopped a short distance away. No one emerged.

He walked nervously over to it. A window came down. *Phut. Phut.* There was a single silenced shot to his chest. The second went into his forehead before he hit the ground. It was the classic professional assassin's double tap. Two men got out of the car. One checked that there was no pulse. They bundled the body into black trash bags, tossed it in the back of the vehicle, and drove off.

3

Child Murderer?

The 50 Carat Diamond restaurant in Manhattan does not exist. It is so exclusive and is impossible to find, except by its ultra-rich, secretive patrons. Its existence has never been proven.

An even more exclusive private dining room was accessed via a hidden elevator. Other than the heavily vetted staff, there were only three people who could book this room. It was swept for electronic surveillance devices three times a day. Multibillion dollar deals, the destinies of countries, and sometimes more important matters, like the purchase of the rarest Bugatti, or of a stolen Picasso that could never be shown in public, were discussed here.

Joel Dolan, dot-com billionaire, and possibly the richest man in the world, if all his secrets were revealed, was enjoying lunch. He had at least fifty private chefs on his yachts, in his private mansions around the world, and on his personal jet fleet. Some were lent out for months on end to national presidents, royal houses, and others he wished to influence. Yet, as he put it, "I like a little variety. So here we are."

He waved a lobster claw menacingly at his public relations advisor who was dining with him. "Look Freddie, I've spent my entire life staying off the publicity grid. Now you're telling me I should stick my head above the parapet. What the hell do I pay you for?"

"Joel we've worked together for fifteen years. As promised back then, still no one has a clue how rich and powerful you are. I think I've done my job."

"So why change anything?"

"Because we live in a world where so much is monitored by the NSA, the FBI, the IRS and others, that leaks can occur. Worse, many tin-pot little countries like France, Israel, and Russia can hack into information from anywhere. One day, leaks will start which we can't stop."

"So, what do you want to do?"

"Simple, we set you up as a minor billionaire as a cover. If any security breaches occur, you're just a bit player. What's all the fuss about? Go track Gates, Bezos, Zuckerberg, and the rest of the bigger fish."

"Freddy, OK you're hired for another year. Where do we start?"

***

The next day, Freddy began to implement the plan. The front page of the New York Times obliged.

Billionaire Philanthropist takes the Plunge

Joel Dolan becomes the latest celebrity to take in a Ukrainian refugee…

He says, "Everyone is touched by the scale of human tragedy. We all must play our part."

There followed a short profile of Daniela Slivka. It focused heavily on how the 40-year-old had been dug out of the ruin of her Kharkiv apartment, after three days buried in the rubble. Then, she was strafed, shot at, and beaten up, as she made her painfully slow way to Romania and safety. Pictures of her bloodied face and bandaged limbs filled the page.

The Times did not add that Dolan was busy making tens of billions from buying up Russian assets cheaply, and from his stock in armaments and oil companies.

***

At 11a.m., May 14, 2023, Daniela was cleaning the inside windows of the Dolans' New York penthouse flat overlooking Central Park. Joel's third trophy wife, tennis champion Barbie Slanger, sipped a second Martini, indolently draped over a sofa. "You missed a bit, Bitch!"

Aaron Aalborg

She liked to see the ladder sway perilously as Daniela struggled to reach the far corner indicated. Six-year-old Sam Dolan laughed nastily. "Missed a bit, lazy Bitch!"

His mother patted him on the head. Daniela was slapped, kicked, and punched almost every day by Barbie. As she curled up on the floor trying to defend herself, little Sam pulled her hair, scratched at her eyes, and tore at her clothes. Daniela was a mass of bruises and contusions. Her right eye was so puffed she could hardly see.

***

The next day, at 10 a.m., Barbie was at her Zumba class in their gym room with her personal coach. Sam's homeschooling was due to start at 10:30. Daniela was vacuuming the priceless silk Persian rug. A gift from the ruler of an oil state

Sam ran across to her, tripping her over. He unclipped the lid on the dust bag, tipping it out. Dust clouded over her and the carpet. He ran up and kicked her hard in the shin. "Get up, Bitch! Wait till Dad sees what you've done."

Choking with dust and rage, she exploded. She scooped him up and threw him out of the open window, fifteen floors up. He screamed as he fell.

By the time NYPD arrived, Barbie had beaten Daniela's face to a bloody pulp.

Ukraine Refugees

Half an hour later Freddie picked up the phone in his smart Park Avenue office. It was a furious Dolan. "What now?– Genius!"

***

Over the next two days Daniela was indicted, chained to a bed in the prison hospital. Reviled by the nurses and doctors, she was a monster, a child killer. She had bitten the hand that fed her. She would die in prison.

***

Freddie sipped a Manhattan, as he waited for Dolan in the 50 Carat Diamond.

Dolan stormed in. A deferential waiter handed him his usual bourbon and branch water, asked if he wanted anything else, and made a discrete exit. Dolan shouted and screamed for nearly ten minutes. Thousands of Dolan's enemies had disappeared or died over the years. "There's not a judge, jury, cop, or warder in the world we can't get to. The numbers men tell me we pay off over 150,000 people around the world, all told. The stairs at Bedford Hills Penitentiary are begging for her to tumble down. I'll have her gutted in there! She'll be found hanged in her cell. Slow poison might be a more painful death."

***

Freddie knew from experience that he needed to let the balloon of his anger deflate. Eventually and in a calm voice he said, "Remember, our objective is to showcase you as a modest, minor, and philanthropic billionaire." He pressed on, as Dolan looked about to burst into a further diatribe. "The best thing is for this story to disappear.

"You'll get sympathy when we place discreet pictures of you and Barbie weeping and clinging together at the funeral. Remember the Lindbergh kid? Daniela'll be quietly declared insane, due to her experiences. She goes to a secure place forever. She'll be so sedated, she might as well be dead. As Barbie can't have further children, she disappears in a yachting accident. You remarry. Simple!"

"Right! I like it. Implement!"

4

Miss Prim and Proper

In February 2022, the north-eastern city of Kharkiv became a battleground. At the start of the invasion there had been about 1.4 million inhabitants. Russian was the common language. Orthodox Christianity was the dominant religion.

Attacks by Russian missiles, artillery and ground troops wrecked the city. Many still survived, sheltering, huddled amongst the wreckage of their homes. Others were fleeing. Their shortest escape route was to Russia. Western countries were a huge distance away.

Kharkiv had been a regional cultural centre with opera, ballet, theatre, and art galleries. To balance this was a thriving night life, bars, brothels, and entertainment for the less cultured.

***

Boyka was strutting from the subway after a 34-minute ride east of the city. She was going to visit her sister in the small rural suburb of Rohan. Her sister was 22, two years her junior. Boyka liked to look her best for such visits, as sisters do.

Boyka had long blond hair in an attractive style. She wore high-heeled blue shoes to match her figure-hugging dress and bright blue eyes. As always, she looked as though she had spent hours before the mirror, using the most fashionable and expensive makeup.

To avoid damaging her shoes, she was treading carefully along the rough approach to her sister's house. All the same, she managed to swing her hips and her expensive handbag. The men in the street gave her appreciative glances. Such beauty and finery were rarely seen in the city, let alone here.

***

Whoosh! Whoosh! Bang! Bang! The row of small houses in front of her exploded and vanished into a cloud of dust and flying debris. She was thrown backwards by the blast and landed on her back, ears ringing. She rolled over, not believing what was happening. She pushed herself up, kicked off her shoes, and ran toward her sister's house.

A missile had landed in the front, blowing in the wall and windows.

Shocked and terrified as to what she might find, she picked her way through fallen beams, broken glass and shattered furniture. Her sister and her infant nephew lay dead on the floor in a rear room. Pathetically, he was holding a torn teddy bear.

She sat on the bed burying her head in her hands. As her mind cleared, she thought, *Must get away from here! More might be coming.*

She was used to difficult situations, but nothing like this. Following her instincts, she opened a wardrobe. As fast as she could, she stripped off her finery, exposing an extremely fit body. She grabbed more practical and duller clothes. *These mean I can move faster. With the Nike trainers I can walk better too.*

She grabbed a pair of scissors, some sausage, and rye bread, shoving them into a shopping bag. *I'll stick this kitchen knife in my belt too. Rape is common in war.*

She ran out the back door, leaving the horror behind. As she left, a burst of heavy machine gun fire stitched across the wall above her head, smashing the bricks. Tracers were flying everywhere. Diving for the frozen earth, she crawled through the frozen ruts of the empty vegetable patch and into a ditch. Peeping through a bush, she saw soldiers running on toward the village.

She hacked off as much of her hair as she could and stayed put until dark. Somewhere, heavy vehicles rumbled past. *What should I do? Staying here isn't possible. I'll freeze to death. How to get away from the fighting? Russia is the closest option. That's where these killers are coming from. I'd better head west toward the city.*

***

It stays light late in these latitudes in winter. Cautiously, she started to walk, with the explosions and gunfire rolling on a good distance ahead of her. *I'd best keep out of sight to the right of the road, ready to hide if they come.*

Around 11 p.m. she came across a massive armored vehicle parked near a roaring fire. Each of its eight black tires dwarfed her. Three men were drinking vodka from a huge bottle and warming themselves. *If I stay behind this hedge, they won't see me. I've got to slip past them.*

One of the three stood up. He staggered over within a few feet of her and urinated. He heard her as she tried to move away. Pulling out his pistol he shouted, "Come out or I shoot!"

His comrades seized their weapons, moving forward.

"Don't shoot! I'm just trying to stay safe." She stood up, raising her hands.

"Well my pretty, you look as if you had a rough day," said the oldest of the three, obviously the leader. "Come and warm yourself. We'll see what you have to say."

Ukraine Refugees

He thrust the vodka bottle into her hands. She took a deep swig of the fiery liquid.

"Hey! Leave some for us," joked another.

They let her spoon some hot soup into a can and started to question her.

***

"I'm a teacher at the local infants' school. I was looking in on a sick pupil. When I got there, the house blew up. The boy and his mother are dead."

She cried and sobbed. She was cold as ice inside, seeing the risks in her situation. The men were quite drunk and threw her a blanket. "Bedtime." Fortunately, they all fell into a drunken sleep around the roaring warmth of the fire.

As they snored, she extracted the knife from her bag. She softly approached the first one. Putting a hand over his mouth, she calmly slit his throat. *That'll teach you to kill my kinfolk!* She dispatched the two others. Washing her hands with vodka, she took what food she could carry, jogging west as fast as she could. *I'll use the road for speed. If I hear or see anything I'll get off it.*

***

The wrecked village school was on her right. She went in to see if there was anything useful. She wished she had not. At least 20 children's bodies were strewn about, many blown to pieces. *Oh god! There's the teacher, clothes torn. She's been raped. Stabbed too. Bastards!*

Calming herself, she looked through a bag on the floor. An ID card showed the teacher was Miss Daryna Andrich. She had been blond. Boya shoved the card in her bag and moved on. Outside was a bicycle to speed her journey.

***

By January 2023, Boyka, now calling herself Daryna Andrich, had used the peace agreement to head west. The chaos, and keeping herself looking a mess, enabled her to pass as Daryna and obtain exit papers. She reached Berlin in February. As she traveled through Eastern Europe on the way to Berlin, she noticed that even the Poles were so much wealthier than Ukrainians. *That's it, I'm never going back.*

She was placed in the household of Dr. Juergen Schierz, the owner of a printing works. She would work as a Putzfrau, to clean his apartment and home office. Frau Schierz would manage her work. The couple had no children.

Because "Daryna" spoke good English like her employers, they gave her instructions in that language. They also started to teach her German. She picked it up fast. Some of her customers back home had been German, so she knew more than she let on.

Ukraine Refugees

Her employers were impressed that she was using words they had not taught her.

This will do for now, but I must plan for better things.

***

Frau Schierz was a stickler for correctness and perfect work. Daryna met her needs as much as anyone could. She had her own room and bathroom in their luxurious high-rise home. *Wow! The Germans are so rich. My maid's quarters are way better than my high-end place in Kharkiv.*

My eyes are opened. I never knew how poor we Ukrainians were. How come the Germans are so rich after they lost the war? They were nearly as bad as Stalin to us. I'll stay here, learn the ropes, and then go my own way.

On her two nights off a week, she looked around Berlin's famous nightlife. Men noticed her and bought her drinks. She fended off their advances with an experienced ease. She saw that the local pole dancers and strippers were no better than she had been at their jobs.

I could do that, but I want more. Much more.

***

Things moved on faster than Daryna expected.

In the swanky Anomalie Art Club, Daryna knew she looked fantastic. She sipped Champagne with a young banker in a shady booth. Through the corner of her eye, she saw a couple enter. She took a closer look. *She's like a hooker. Oh my God! She's with Herr Doktor Schierz.*

She hid her face with a hand for a second. *He's too enthralled with the tart to notice me. What to do? See where they go and blackmail him? Too risky. I know what I'll do.*

Temporarily excusing herself from her partner, she sashayed over to their table. "Guten Abend Herr Schierz." *Ha! The poor chap nearly dropped his beer.*

He regained his composure a little. "Fräulein Andrich, how nice to see you."

The hooker looked annoyed. Daryna apologized for disturbing them and returned to her banker.

How will he play it tomorrow?

***

Daryna was cleaning the house, looking slightly more glamorous than usual. Frau Schierz was enjoying her weekly Kaffee und Torte mit Schlagsahne with her friends in a downtown café.

Usually, Schierz was out when she cleaned his office. Today, he sat behind his big desk as she entered. Unsurprised, she gave him a sweet smile. "Guten Morgen, Doktor."

Ukraine Refugees

He replied in English. "Well Daryna, we need to have a little talk."

He slid a fat envelope across the table. "Open it please."

Looking him in the eyes and still smiling, she pulled the flap. Inside were at least 10,000 Euros in large bills. "Oh, I couldn't possibly accept this." She pushed the envelope back across the desk.

He looked worried. "Then what do you want?"

She swung her hips as she walked around the desk, moving closer to him, so he could smell her perfume. In a husky voice she breathed into his ear, "I want you to take me as your mistress."

Not giving him time to react, she pressed her breast into his face, feeling for his arousal with her hand. He was lost.

In coming weeks, every time Frau Schierz was out, he was in his home office. On his wife's nights off, they went to a Gasthaus in a different part of Berlin.

He told her, "You're the best lover I ever had."

She smiled at the compliment. *You'll never escape my web now. You know what happens to male spiders.*

***

Five years later, Daryna sat in what was now her home office. She was dictating what she wanted on the next supervisory board agenda to her manager at the print works.

It transpired that she was a first-rate businesswoman. Profits had doubled since she took over from her late husband, Juergen. His first wife had died suddenly of a stroke. He was found drowned in the River Spree two years afterwards. He had been drinking very heavily.

She walked over to the mirror and smiled at herself. *You worked hard for all this, but it was worth it.*

5

The Iron Chancellor, Bounder the Dog, and a Poor Orphan

Otto Von Bismarck, famously said, "Fools learn by experience. I prefer to learn from the experience of others."

***

Zaporizhzhia is a city in south-eastern Ukraine, on the banks of the Dnieper River. Before the invasion, its population was just under 750,000. Its metals and other heavy industries used nuclear generated electricity. The power plant made the city the Russian 22nd Army's primary objective in its armored thrust from the adjacent Crimea.

The nuclear plant was famously surrendered with little fighting. This avoided the risk to the whole of Europe and the world of another Chernobyl

Whilst the media focused on the nuclear threat, the fate of the city's orphanages was initially ignored. Ukraine had over 100,000 orphans at the start of the conflict. Charitable and religious organizations and individuals worked hard to save those in danger. Most of those from Zaporizhzhia were evacuated to the Polish border.

In a horrible war, the children evoked special sympathy. Offers to take them poured in.

***

Janet Gazinski and her husband Andrew were comfortably off, lawyers. They lived with their two children, Stephan and John, in a large house in Hampstead, North London.

Both the grandfathers came to Britain from Poland, during World War II. In consequence, Andrew and Janet were well aware of the horrors of war and Russian oppression. They watched the nightly BBC news with mounting distress and heartfelt empathy. She groaned, "We must do something. There's no choice."

He agreed, "But what?"

***

A year earlier, Janet and Andrew's children wanted a dog. Their parents grew up without dogs and so were nervous about the idea. Andrew's father always argued, "We need the food for our family. Feeding a dog isn't going to happen."

Ukraine Refugees

Eager to please her boys, Janet discussed the idea with friends in her city law firm. She did not like some of the stories.

"Belinda, our oldest, wanted a dog. My husband insisted on no puppies, because of the house training issues. We went to a rescue center. Belinda fell in love with the cutest little King Charles spaniel. She called her Bright Eyes. We had problems from day one. The damned dog pooped everywhere all the time. The animal was terrified of anyone except me. The last straw was when it bit the baby. "We found out it had been neglected and abused. We took it back. They offered another, but once bitten, twice shy."

Andrew's online research threw up even worse cases. From a dog training site, "Any child psychologist will tell you that abused or neglected children are deeply traumatized. A minority become psychotic and child abusers themselves. It's the same with dogs."

A reply to this post, "We brought home an adorable puppy. It had some cuts and bruises. He seemed very fearful. My wife and daughter wanted to mother him. We named him Bounder. Bounder went crazy anytime anyone came to see us. We were all bitten. He savaged and tore any soft furnishings he could get his teeth into. Our furniture was wrecked.

"One morning, he jumped up and clamped onto my daughter's neck. I bashed him with a stick till he let go. She was hospitalized. Bounder was put down. Never again!"

Reply from the site sponsors, "We are sorry for your experiences and understand your feelings. We must point out that such cases are rare. The vast majority of rescue dogs are loving and happy in their new homes. Do try again. You can save a good dog from being put down."

Janet and Andrew agreed. No dogs!

***

Many Ukrainian children in orphanages are classed as "social orphans." Their parents suffer temporary hardships. The families usually recover them. With the war this was difficult.

Vadin was a seven-year-old in a Zaporizhzhia orphanage when the invasion began. Handwritten notes in his file included, "Father died instantly. Killed by exploding metal in the Melitposkyy Zavod foundry… Mother committed suicide… Before he arrived here aged three, he was taken in by a sister and badly neglected…"

A child psychology website states that, "Babies that are never picked up, cuddled, or spoken too can be affected for life… They commonly exhibit some, or all of the following symptoms: rocking back and forth, bed wetting, late mental development, inability to speak, learning difficulties, extreme anger tantrums, inability to form relationships, violence against caregivers or other children, cannot distinguish between acceptable and unacceptable behavior… Frequently, they become sociopathic before adulthood."

***

Vadin exhibited most of these symptoms. He rarely spoke, but he was exceptionally intelligent. In addition, he seemed impervious to pain, perhaps due to the many beatings he received as an infant. The other children learned to avoid him or to suffer the consequences.

Before they were evacuated, he saw the panic caused by the approaching Russian army. He heard the gunfire and explosions coming closer. When the children were herded to shelter, he hid. *I want to see the explosions.* From the window he saw a tank crushing a car. Next it blew the side off the building opposite. A woman was cut down by machine gun fire.

He was excited and wanted more.

***

The same day, the Russians agreed that the orphans be bused west. The other children looked terrified, obeying instructions, standing in line for the bus and clutching their bags.

Vadin dropped his pack. He ran from the line to explore the area before a Russian soldier dragged him back, kicking and screaming. Later, the soldier checked his grenades. *Is one missing?*

***

The bus took days to reach the crossing point to Poland at Przemyśl. During the journey Vadin relished the destruction and distress. The others hid below the windows.

Long after the bus and many other vehicles had passed through a Russian checkpoint, a soldier discovered the loss of his pistol. Vadin was enjoying himself. *Maybe I could be a Russian soldier and drive a tank?*

At Lviv on the Ukraine side, they disembarked to be fed and rested. Russian munitions rocked the area. A smaller blast from a grenade wounded some people nearby. The defenders did not know how any Russians could be so close. It caused a panic. The rest stop was curtailed.

***

Janet and Andrew were delighted that out of more than 150,000 Brits seeking to house refugees, they were of the less than 20,000 chosen, especially as their desire for an orphan was granted. The process was protracted and seemed unnecessarily bureaucratic.

Andrew collected an unsmiling Vadin by taxi.

He spoke slowly, tapping his chest. "Andrew." He pointed to the boy. "You?"

No response. After six tries, Vadin was bored by the fool. "Vadin."

With scowling ill grace, Vadin accepted his own room for the first time in his life, the new clothes, the unpleasant meal, and the greetings of the two boys. The boys showed him around the house. He noted things of value, escape routes and combustibles. They left him alone after he thumped one of them.

Just after midnight, he crept down the stairs, took a deep swig of Janet's Bombay Gin, and implemented his plan. The house was far enough away from the neighbors for the four shots to go unheard.

Vadin hid in some bushes, savoring the sirens, the flashing lights, the animated silhouettes of the men fighting the blaze, the crackling of the flames, the acrid smell of the smoke, the collapsing roof, and other delightful details. His heart beat faster.

He hefted his bag. It was heavier now. The additional weight comprised Janet's jewelry, the contents of Andrew's wallet, some bread and cheese, a bottle of scotch – oh, and a plastic tank from the toy box. The pistol was tucked in the back of his belt, under his jacket. He walked off across Hampstead Heath, clinging to the shadows. He paused in the cover of some bushes.

I like this country. Few people carry guns. The locals seem naïve, ready for my domination.

6

A Recruit for the CIA

Handheld Stinger missiles can shoot down the latest Russian jets and helicopters at close range. They were game changers in Afghanistan. Here, they could allow a successful defense of Mariupol against the overwhelming Russian airpower and 22nd Army.

A shipment of stingers arrived from NATO sources in Mariupol on February 21. Knowledge of the delivery was on a need-to-know basis. Without delay, crack national guard soldiers were receiving the simple training needed to deploy and fire them in a secret warehouse location.

***

On the 24th of February, the Russians began their drive on Mariupol from nearby Crimea. As dawn broke, a squadron of aircraft dropped laser-guided bombs in a low-level attack on the warehouse. The stingers, trained men, and volunteer instructors were wiped out.

***

Aaron Aalborg

In the Ukraine army HQ, the commander demanded, "How did they know? We have a traitor somewhere in our inner circle!"

They looked at each other with suspicion. One member of the team congratulated himself on a job well done.

***

Mariupol, February 29, 2022. – I've been separated from my Ukrainian National Guard unit for three days. I'm surrounded by Russians. We were formerly known as the Azov Regiment, far right anti-Russian shock troops. They give us the jobs the regulars cannot do. If they want every living thing wiped out, we're the boys to do it.

I'm known as, "Khaker, the Hacker" because I can hack into anyone's IT.

I think I'm one of the meanest, toughest bastards in my unit. For two days I've been holed up on the 6th floor of a shattered apartment block. The people've all fled,

My wounded shoulder still aches in the freezing nights. Mmm, it's a while since they put me back in the line. Maybe there are still splinters in there.

Scavenging for food and other things from the apartments is easy. The owners left with what they could carry. There's enough to eat and other stuff to keep me going for a while. I must be careful. I nearly fell down a big hole in the floor this morning.

My sniper rifle is propped against the wall. It's the latest NATO model. I've killed a few people with it in the last two days. Two were Ukrainian fighters. They really shouldn't send untrained people into combat. They don't even know how to take cover. The other was an old woman who looked up. I think she saw me. Got her, right between the eyes.

Hell! Some Ukrainians are searching the apartments. They'll be here in a few minutes.

***

"Hey! Anyone up here better surrender or we'll blow you to hell."

I'll shove the rifle under this bed, then raise my hands.

"Don't shoot. I'm one of you. I've been operating under cover. You need to inform Colonel Sverdlov that you've found me – immediately."

Three very suspicious soldiers kept me covered. None too gently, they shepherded me down to their unit commander. After a conversation on the radio, they put me into a light vehicle a little more deferentially. Thus, I spent a week, off the radar, in a Russian headquarters.

***

Top Secret – Extracts from transcripts of the interrogation of Vasilko Shevchenko, aka, "Khaker the Hacker." Conducted by agent Y in our secure site in Latvia,[4] March to April 2023:

"Tell us how you became associated with the Azov Battalion."

"I joined the Social Nationalist Assembly (SNA) in 2009 because of their anti-Russian stance…

"Before that I worked with a group of computer hackers to infiltrate and damage Russian Federation sites…

"Yes, I'm a white supremacist. It's self-evident we were born to rule. Look at the state of the countries run by other races. It's self-evident that US foreign policy is decided in Israel. You must know that. In Ukraine we deal with that type of problem."

"Yes, that's me in a video, holding down a Roma man. A comrade is beating him with a baseball bat…

"In 2014 I joined the successor, Azov regiment…

---

[4] Poland and the Baltic NATO countries were among the places the CIA had black sites. They were used to house prisoners during or after extraordinary rendition from other countries. "Enhanced interrogation," including water boarding, was conducted there.

Ukraine Refugees

"I trained to fight separatists in the Donbas region…

"We slaughtered any Russians we could get, men, women, and children...

"We recaptured Mariupol from the Russian stooges in the same year. I was wounded in the shoulder by grenade splinters.

"We played an important role in overthrowing the government and installing one we liked better….

"We were incorporated into the Ukrainian National guard as a shock unit, shortly afterward. I was in hospital at the time

"In 2016, I returned to the front lines in Donbas liquidating opponents…

"Since 2018 I have helped the leadership in the computer intelligence team."

***

May 2023, in the Office of the Deputy Director for Operations of the CIA, Langley, Virginia:

"What's your take on this guy, Ted?"

"We need to tread carefully, Sir.

"He passed all the polygraphs, but trained people can do that. Our shrinks say he's unusually manipulative and very hard to read. They recommend we don't use him.

"His white supremacist and personal involvement in the murder of women civilians is a ticking time bomb. We don't know who else has the dirt on Schevchenko under his various aliases. On the other hand, he knows the key players personally, has an inside track to his group, which has gone underground in the new regime. He could be a useful asset."

"What's your bottom line?"

"We use him but have firewalls between his handlers and us."

"Humph. Our policy's always been to bury their past if the bad guys can help us defeat the enemy. That's how we got to the moon and won the last cold war. Some of the nastiest Nazis had spy networks in the East. Of course, we always had a hold over them.

"Go for it!"

***

A coded message arrived in the Moscow HQ of the SVR, the CIA's counterpart.

"I am in!"

7

A Normal Family

February 2022 – Évian-les-Bains is a delightful spa town in northern Haute-Savoie, France. It overlooks Lake Geneva. Partly wooded, there are fields with dairy cattle. Mont Blanc and the Alps are a short drive away. The famous Evian Water is bottled there and exported worldwide, to the chagrin of environmentalists.

56-year-old Jacques Dubois had lived all his life in a large house in a village on the edge of the town with his mother, 92-year-old Madame Christine. His wife, Solange, his troublesome 15-year-old daughter, Marie-Claude, and his son of 14, Pierre, shared the Swiss chalet style wooden house. It had eight bedrooms, a patio with a carved balustrade, and splendid views. In the summer, red geraniums cascaded down from the balcony. Jacques owned a white-water rafting business on the River Dranse in nearby Thonon-les Bains for the summer tourist season. He rented his fields to a local dairy farm.

His deportment and appearance mimicked the regional mascot, the nervous, hardy, and busy marmot. A large, furry rodent, it is ever alert for eagles and other predators, ready to dive down the nearest hole if one of its colony squeaks an alarm.

Jacque's mother was a traditional Catholic. She often admonished the family with threats of impending hell-fire for what she considered their modern views. She lamented the replacement of Latin mass with French.

His wife, Solange, was well liked in the area. Still attractive, she was pleasant to everyone. She taught at the local primary school.

Marie-Claude was developing into an extremely attractive young woman. She resented the limitations of the French Government's COVID policies on her sparse, off-season, social life. She could hardly wait to escape to Paris or Lyons for her higher education.

Pierre spent most of his spare time playing video games with his school friends on the internet. He had a crush on his art teacher, blushing whenever she entered the classroom.

***

The Ukraine war led to wildly different reactions. Marie-Claude and Pierre were uninterested. Solange was upset at the bloody, broken bodies and streams of refugee children. Madame Christine was of two minds. The priest in the local church, explained, "Most Ukrainians are Catholics. The Russian invaders are either atheists or heretic Orthodox."

Collections were taken for aid. Madame Christine remembered the problems of Algerian immigration in France.

"I'm just glad they stay in the big cities."

Jacques surprised them all with the vehemence of his reaction. "We have to help!"

His wife agreed. She smiled at him, *He's a good man.*

He silenced his mother with, "It's your Christian duty, remember the Good Samaritan. What would Jesus do?"

He and Solange discussed what they could do. It was the off season for tourists.

***

March 2022 – Nykolai Kovalenko had discussed emigrating from the Ukraine for some years. His wife, Tatiana, worked in a run-down Kyiv factory. She hated it. He was employed in poorly paid manual jobs. He was muscular and handsome. The president was blocking men from fleeing the capital. "All must fight to save our homeland."

"To hell with that! We're getting out of here."

The local boys all sought the company of their daughter, Elena. She had a reputation for being obliging.

16-year-old Alexandr had inherited his father's good looks. "I don't want to fight either. How'll we get out?"

***

Despite their low pay, the family could afford a small van. The loan was funded by Tatiana turning the odd trick. Nykolai duped a widow out of some money, pretending to be unmarried. Petty thefts supplemented his income. Elena sold herself too. Alexandr pushed cannabis at the local school. So far, they had stayed out of the hands of the law. Besides, the cops had their hands full now.

They loaded up their luggage. Nykolai said, "They say there are ten million displaced from their homes. That's a quarter of our population. No one will have much time to check every vehicle. Alexandr and I'll hide under a pile of blankets and bags when we leave. Same applies passing through inhabited areas. If anyone asks, tell 'em we went south to fight in Mariupol."

Tatiana and Elena made a point of packing sexy clothes and makeup.

"If needed, we'll give the eye to anyone who stops us."

***

Late March 2022 – Jacques loaded his blue Renault Trafic van with supplies for the refugees. Normally he used it to ferry up to eight tourists from the airport or around the sights. There were diapers, food, fruit juice, tinned food, and baby formula. He added a jerry can of spare diesel and some containers of engine oil too. *I'll pack a one-man tent in case I can't find a place to stay. There's no space to sleep in the van. It's so full.*

Solange was worried. "It's such a long drive Jacques. Will the Renault make it? What if you break down?"

"I've got my cell phone. The route is on main roads."

"Oh, I love you so much. You're my hero. Bon chance!"

More reluctantly, the rest of the family came out to wave him off.

He headed down the drive. *It'll be an adventure.*

***

His route skirted Switzerland, passing through Bavaria, the Czech Republic, and Slovakia to reach the Polish border. The news, and Waze on his cell phone, helped him reach the transit point. It took him four days. Exhausted, he donated all the supplies to the locals. The Poles were well organized. He left the tent too. He had not needed it en route.

He expected to drive straight back with a full load of eight refugees. He held up his sign,
"Eight People – France."

He was surprised. People were traveling on coaches. Others boarded trains. A few had their own vehicles. He spoke to a fellow Good Samaritan from Lille. He looked despondent. "I've been waiting two days. No one wants to come with me. Everyone either wants to stay close, so they can return home soon, or they are on trains and coaches to other places."

Jacques was amazed. Day after day he held up his sign.

***

Ukraine Refugees

As they neared the border, Nykolai pulled off the road.

"We'll dump the car, crossing the Polish border unofficially. The map shows some woods. We'll circle back to the legal crossing point on the Polish side. We'll find a way forward after that."

His wife and daughter were angry at the thought of lugging their luggage through rough countryside. "What about our car?" Challenged Tatiana.

"Not to worry. It isn't ours. We haven't paid for it. We can always steal another later."

***

They reached the Polish side, dirty and weary. Nykolai exclaimed, "Hey look! There's a guy with a van. He's offering a ride to France."

Elena brightened. "Paris. I've always wanted to go there."

Jacques was so pleased to see them he forgot about fully loading the Renault. They set off, just the five of them. They could not believe their luck. Jacques paid for all the guest houses and meals on the way.

Alexandr nudged his father, "See that wad of Euros and all the credit cards in his wallet."

As they passed through prosperous Bavaria, Nykolai commented. "We've definitely made the right decision."

***

They drove into the countryside of Haute-Savoie, Jacques' home department. As he pulled into the drive of the large house, Elena's face dropped. "Oh no! This isn't Paris. It looks like a farm."

Her father noticed the Peugeot 208 and Citroen C5 in front of the garage. He remarked, "Relax it will be fine, for now. These people are rich."

Alerted by cell phone, the whole family came out to greet the filthy van. Wizened and diminutive, Madame Christine was grim-faced. She looked them over disapprovingly. Solange beamed. Spying Alexandr, Marie-Claude perked up. Pierre blushed as the stunning Elena swung her shapely legs out of the van. They rushed to help unload.

"Wow! Will you look at this place." said Alexandr.

"It's still not Paris," remarked, Elena, giving Pierre her sexiest smile and brushing back her hair.

***

The next morning, the village priest brought Evgenia as an interpreter. She had worked as a cleaner in one of the spa hotels for 20 years. Even she noticed how handsome and strong Nykolai was.

With Evgenia's help they exchanged rudimentary information. "I worked as a driver," said Nykolai.

"I rented my own boutique," claimed Tatiana. "It was all bombed out. We lost everything."

They explained that the French food was strange. Evgenia agreed to help them buy more palatable fare.

***

By May, the tourists had returned. Jacques was out much of the time. When he was at home, and Solange was not in the room, Tatiana stood as close to him as she could. To begin with, he was uncomfortable, but now he rather liked it. Pierre had abandoned his video games so he could spend all his non-school time gazing at Elena.

Nykolai explained his master plan to his family. "Elena, you will seduce Pierre and get pregnant. They'll have to keep us here. Tatiana, you move in on Jacques. I'll try Solange. Alexandr can befriend Marie-Claude. We'll get control of this place, sell it, and move to Paris."

Nykolai began work as a driver for Jaques. He ferried tourists from the airport and to white water rafting. Jaques said, "We'll teach you rafting soon."

"I'd be nervous. I can't swim."

Elena helped around the house. She cooked for the Ukrainians. It was a puzzle to the French. "How anyone could like this stuff."

The villagers were supportive. The men took to surreptitiously ogling the women from their games of Pétanque

***

Madame Christine was scandalized when she saw Elena emerging from Pierre's room. Elena gave her a knowing smile and moved on.

She told Jacques the minute he returned home.

"Don't be silly mother. He's only a schoolboy."

To her surprise, Solange started to have feelings for Nykolai. She saw him washing in the yard. His handsome looks and rippling muscles were a far cry from Jacques'. A day later, he caught her round the waist and swung her to him. She tried to push him away. His hot breath was in her ear. He kissed her on the lips. She struggled free, heart racing. She rushed out of the room.

Should she tell Jacques? Better not. Besides, she kept thinking how nice it was.

***

By the end of May, Pierre was spending more time in Elena's room than his own. His mother had succumbed to Nykolai. Alexandr was seen by Madame Christina in a passionate kiss with Marie-Claude.

Madame Christina went to the village priest, as did the rest of her family. They did so under the seal of silence in the confessional. The Sunday sermon railed against the iniquities of adultery and lust. The villagers seemed a bit surprised. As old Georges commented after the service, "After all, we are French."

His friend Alan replied, "He must have held some interesting confessions this week."

***

Madame Christine tripped and fell down the stairs. Distraught, Jaques visited her in hospital. She was not expected to live. The priest pulled him aside for a quiet word. He told Jacques what she had confided in him. It was not a confession, so he could. Jaques was relaxed until he heard that Solange was having an affair with Nikolai.

He was furious. Blinding anger was followed by cold blooded scheming. *Something has to be done.*

"Nikolai, it's time you learned white water rafting."

The next day he took the Ukrainian along with Jean, his regular boat skipper. "I'll steer." He told a surprised Jean. It had been a few years since he did that job.

The river was not that dangerous. To heighten the thrills, Jean often tipped his visitors into the rushing water. As long as he picked his spot to pitch them out of the boat, and they wore their cork vests and protective helmets, they could be safely brought to shore.

Nikolai looked worried. He muttered, "I can't swim."

Jacques reached up to personally fasten his safety gear. "I remember, you told me before. We'll look after you. Don't worry."

The rubber boat swirled away down the rapids. In the bow of the dinghy, Jean sat at one side to fend off the rocks with his paddle. Nikolai was at the other. He was terrified. Jacques steered from the stern with another oar. The boat pitched and bumped. It swirled and spun. Nikolai was petrified.

"Wake up! Push off the rocks!" bellowed Jean.

Jacques had not lost his touch. He picked his moment well. The boat spun – Alex was thrown out. He banged his head hard on a huge rock. His loosely fastened helmet tore off. Other rocks followed. Jacques rolled out of the dinghy. He swam to Alex, ensuring his head stayed under the water.

An old hand, Jean focused on staying in the boat, looking straight ahead. It was carried rapidly downstream.

***

The two funerals were on separate days. The whole village turned out. Madame Christine had traditional, black-plumed horses.

Nikolai was a simpler affair.

In December, Pierre was last seen boarding a train for the capital. He was never seen again.

8

Following in Great Granma's Footsteps

Lydmyla gave this testimony to the investigators:

"My great grandmother, Kuzma, told us how, in 1933, most of our family died. They were farmers during what we call the 'Holodomor.' That was our time of starvation, brutality, and death. For Great Granma it meant misery, then exile for many miserable years.

"At first, the family hoped that collective farms would give peasants like them the chance to be better off. The administrators promised new tractors, more animals and better crop yields. Initially they sent city people from Russia to help work the fields. Many were enthusiastic idealists and students. The family hoped that Bolshevism might end interminable generations of drudgery.

"The communist apparatchiks supervised the liquidation of those who used to own the bigger farms. They were rebellious and resentful. Kuzma's menfolk felt this was a necessary step. There was pity for their innocent families. They were told the children would be sent to families in the cities, or orphanages. Moscow imposed heavier and heavier production quotas. The animals were slaughtered. The meat was taken away. Some in the Kuzma's family were shot for concealing meat. Then the harvest failed, just before an especially harsh winter.

"At exactly this time, when there was insufficient to eat on the farms, Stalin exported what wheat there was to pay for his military and other projects in hard currency. A deliberate policy of starving the peasants began.

"Old Kuzma told us how, in 1933, the police ransacked their home for anything edible. They even stole the small pieces of bread from the children's hands. In the next few days, children and adults starved, one-by-one. She tried to give away her youngest baby when her milk dried up, but the neighbors were dying too. Some were eating their own relatives. She cried when she told us this. She ate rats. Too weak to bury the last to die, she had only managed to drag the bodies out to freeze outside.

"The police came again. She was the only one left. They claimed she had been hiding food. They must have had a quota to fill. They bundled her into a vehicle, then with others, they were forced up into a windowless freezing cattle truck on the railway to Russia.

"There were many more deaths during a nightmare journey. She worked in the frozen wastes of a gulag near Jakoetsk in Eastern Siberia for many years, barely surviving. Suicide was a common cause of death.

"A year after Khrushchev became First Secretary of the Party, she was ordered back to Ukraine, without explanation. She met her second husband in the train carriage on the long journey back."

***

"I was working as a teacher's assistant in the nursery school my small daughter attended in Kherson. Our town was a thriving Black Sea port. It was the first day's objective for the invading Russian army. It was part of their route to our bigger port and naval base of Odessa. My husband had gone there to help defend the city a few days earlier.

"We had no defence. We were attacked with bombs and artillery. Russian armor drove into the city.

"We were hiding in a cellar when they banged on the door. We cowered against the walls. The soldiers seemed to think we would be friendly. I thought they needed history lessons. They informed us we would be taken to Russia the next day.

Ukraine Refugees

"The following afternoon, several hours late, a huge six-wheel truck roared into the square. It had large white Zs daubed on the front and back. They told us we would be cared for. They carried guns, so we were worried. They helped the women up onto the truck, then handed up our children. We saw helicopters flying overhead. Explosions shook the ground and rumbled in the distance. We just wanted to escape."

***

"Things changed across the Russian border.

"We were taken into a school. An officious officer demanded our papers. Then the questions began:

'Where's your husband?'

'He went to Odessa to work.'

'Are you sure he's not in the army?'

"After that, the people were less friendly. Half of us were moved out in a bus and taken to a station.

"Two days later, following a change of trains, we were put off in Serov. This is a small town, built around its iron industry, in the middle of Russia. We were kept on camp beds in an old military barracks, never allowed out.

"There were armed guards at the gate and a high barbed wire fence. There was only cold water. The food was basic. The toilets were filthy. So were our clothes. We had lice. When my daughter was sick, no one came to attend her.

"After a few months, things suddenly changed. They brought better food. A doctor checked those with health problems. We were shown films explaining the benefits of living in the Russian Federal Republic. We were taken to a desk in a big room one at a time. A secretary gave us vodka or tea.

"The official said these things:

'We would be pleased to offer you asylum in Russia...

'Your skills in childcare are needed...

'We can pay you far more than you were getting in Ukraine...

'Much of your country was destroyed by the fascists in the government. There is nothing to return to...

'We can help find your relatives and bring them back to live with you here...

'As your husband left you, there are many handsome men with good jobs looking for wives In Russia...'

"When they saw that all of us wanted to go home, they finally shipped us back as part of the peace agreement.

Ukraine Refugees

"How could I stay? It would have been a dishonor to Great Granma Kuzma, to my parents, to my husband, and to our history.

"My husband is still missing"

9

Never Forget

Maidan Nezalezhnosti, or Independence Square, in Kyiv, is the focal point for all important ceremonies. It was one of the first areas to be cleaned up after the signing of the peace agreement. Hundreds of citizens formed human chains to move the rubble. The army helped. Then the heavy machinery came in as part of the international aid program.

Architects improved some buildings, but the new government did not want to lose the feel of what was there before. It symbolized the sense of nationhood, struggle, and victory. The scars of bullets and shrapnel were deliberately left on some of the buildings as an important reminder of the war.

Naturally, the memorial bearing the names of all the fallen military heroes was built in the square. Because citizens and foreign volunteers took up arms or gave medical care, their dead were recorded there too.

***

The inauguration of the monument was long awaited. The preparations took weeks. Constructing viewing stands and ensuring that the foreign leaders were seated in the right order of precedence was a complex process. The red carpets, rehearsing the military bands, and drilling of the soldiers, sailors, and the air force, took weeks to prepare.

Around the world, speeches were written for the leaders. Security services fretted over the risks to their people. Petty squabbles between the hosts and the US Secret Service over the tiniest details were resolved.

***

Just one name amongst the thousands remembered on the memorial was Sergeant Lyaksandro Kovalenko of the National Guard, formerly of the Azov Battalion. He was shot in the head by a sniper. It was in the last days of the war, as the Russian Army was pulling back from the area around Kyiv.

Now, on this big day, his wife Maria was among the ranks of the honor guard. As the band played the national anthem, many in the crowd wept. Most had lost loved ones or had seen homes and lives devastated.

Maria stood to attention, looking straight ahead. Her blue eyes had a cold glitter. Her heart was ice. Her brain seethed with anger. *The Russians mustn't get away with this. Despite the declarations of victory for democracy from the US and NATO, those cursed animals have won too much.*

When the speeches started, Maria had intended to shoot at the Ukrainian traitors on the rostrum along with the US delegation. *They're the guilty ones in this.*

That idea was thwarted when the US Secret Service demanded that all Ukrainians present would bear deactivated weapons for the ceremony. They would be carefully searched. *That's the ultimate humiliation. It tells who is really running this country now.*

***

Lyaksandro's AZOV Battalion had fought in the Donbas region since 2014. *Now the reds dominate areas in the east, drenched in the blood of our heroes. Pretending the puppet leaders there are part of our new constitution is a joke.*

Our president signed that we won't join NATO. The EU concocted some formula. Without saying so, it stops us joining the trading bloc. They never wanted millions of impoverished Ukrainians to flood their workforce in the first place. Klaus, the German trade unionist who fought alongside me, told me right out.

"The rich EU countries think they have enough cheap labor with the Turks, Romanians, Slovaks, Bulgarians and North Africans. The last thing they want is more. Even my trade union is worried about Ukrainians undercutting the high wages we've negotiated."

Ukraine Refugees

*This war cannot end. It **mustn't end** until Moscow and St. Petersburg are in smoking ruins and every Russian man, woman, and child is dead.*

***

In 2018 Maria and Lyaksandro were at an AZOV reunion. They had met on an earlier National Guard exercise. Six months later they were married. Many Azov leaders came to the wedding.

At that reunion, her eyes shone with excitement as she listened to the impassioned speeches. Her pulse raced. Her man was part of this group. He was strong and loyal. The whole hall had a sense of rampant maleness. She breathed it in. She soaked up the speeches.

"For hundreds of years, Ukrainians have been enslaved by the Russians. They are the ignorant spawn of the Mongol hoards, led by exploiters."

"Underneath they are all killers, rapists, child molesters, and worse."

"Putin's Russia is just a continuation of the murderer Stalin's."

"Will we accept it?"

The men roared back. "No!"

***

On leave from his unit, Lyaksandro told her how he had personally cleansed a leftist village. His eyes lit up. "We rounded up entire families of reds, hitting them with our gun butts and kicking them till they huddled together. We dragged the men out. We beat them, then shot them with our pistols. The women, children, and old people we herded into their schismatic Orthodox church.

"We burnt it to the ground with them in it. My men drank a vodka toast as they screamed."

She found these revelations right and fitting. She was wet with desire. They made hot love in their fever of hate.

***

2023 – The high-tech weapons were collected from Ukrainian units throughout the country by the peacekeeping force. The central depot contained thousands of the hand-held missiles that had proved so devastating to the Russian tanks and helicopters. Crates of rifles, machine guns, grenades, and mines were stacked floor to ceiling. The Russians had taken most of their equipment with them when they pulled back. What was left behind occupied another part of the warehouse.

The perimeter was protected by high fences, razor wire, electronic surveillance, and flood lighting. Armed guards and dogs patrolled the fence. At the corners, watch towers were manned by troops with

Ukraine Refugees

infrared sights. The peacekeepers were confident that no one could get in. Even if they could, swift response units with armored vehicles and helicopters could be on site within minutes.

***

The training camp was hidden in the Slovakian Veľká Fatra Mountains, a part of the Carpathians. It occupied a heavily camouflaged location away from the National Park. Ukrainians were training alongside Slovaks, Czechs, Hungarians, and Poles. Maria Kovalenko was showing a recruit how to operate a US built Stinger anti-aircraft missile. Like the twenty others there, she was under a code name. Hers was '"Claw." The leader was "Dragon," a white supremacist, ex-Navy Seal from Alabama.

The missiles, and more weapons than they could ever need, including C4 plastic explosives for bombs, were easily obtainable. There was no need to raid the arms collected and guarded so diligently by the peacekeepers.

Many Ukrainians had hidden weapons and equipment of all sorts. They did not want to be caught unprepared if the Russians returned. False walls in barns even concealed armored vehicles or heavy artillery.

White supremacist groups in the US and Europe provided all the funding needed. These were especially strong in Germany and Poland.

***

Security was tight. On the third day after this group's arrival, Dragon had a Czech dragged in front of them all. Claw had reported he was using an illicit cell phone to call his woman.

Dragon had been merciless in the interrogation. Truth was he enjoyed it. The man was battered and bleeding. His arm was broken.

Dragon looked each recruit in the eye. "We're all at risk here. There are no second chances."

Phut! The silenced pistol blew the back of the man's head off. No one batted an eyelid.

Claw was singled out for special attention after that. In a Bavarian safe house to learn advanced skills, she received further radicalization. "Our overall objective is to reopen the war with Russia. This time we'll make sure everyone joins in."

"Makes sense. I want to be part of it."

***

So it was that Claw and seventeen others were behind a barn, under nets, hidden in the Donbas region. The heavy vehicle carrying the Russian Pantir anti-aircraft missile system was standing by. Their agent sent a coded text.

"The American Airlines Plane is taking off from Kyiv. The route is confirmed. The manifest shows 122

Ukraine Refugees

US citizens on board. They include the families of two senior CIA agents. Among the non-Americans are families of some NATO generals."

Claw's team left it till the last minute before painting the airliner with their radar.

They fired the missile and tracked it till the blips met on the screen and vanished. Debris and body parts fell over a wide area. Leaving the massive vehicle, all the equipment, and lots of evidence of Russian presence, they headed in different directions on motorcycles.

A nice touch was added to the plan on Claw's suggestion. Two captured Spatznez officers with their documentation were sedated. They were left to be partially incinerated by the missile launch.

As Claw roared away, she was exhilarated.

If the Russians manage to explain their way out of this, one of our other plans will finish the job.

10

Hope for Recovery

August 2023 – Andreas Bischoff was an Emeritierter Wirtschafts professor at a leading German University. He had written several books about the German Post World War II growth miracle. He followed them with publications and broadcasts, explaining the problems of East Germany after the collapse of the Berlin wall.

Below are edited transcripts from an interview he gave about the Ukraine on DW television news:[5]

"Professor, how rapidly do you think it will take the Ukraine economy to bounce back, now that we appear to have peace?"

"Ha! I bring messages of hope, unless something else happens. Let us assume that the agreements reached will be sustained. Unfortunately, this has rarely been true in other cases worldwide. But perhaps peace and prosperity are now in everyone's interests.

---

[5]As this is a novel, the author amalgamated the views of many learned economists into those of the entirely fictional Professor Bischoff.

"The US is under the least pressure because it is self-sufficient in energy, and not far off that in food. Sanctions against Russian energy production and transmission hit Germany the most. Europe, as a whole, has been hardest hit by Russia, taking the Ukraine out of the equation until recovery can be achieved.

"We should start by reviewing where the Ukrainian economy was before the war. Keeping it simple, it was an undeveloped country compared to the rest of mainstream Europe. There are many measures that could be used. We will use gross domestic product per person for simplicity. That means the total amount produced by a country, divided by the population. It is not a number I use much, but the data are stark enough, without the complications of more sophisticated measures.

"Each Ukrainian had a gross domestic product per head in 2020 of only about $3,800. Neighboring Poland generated $15,700 per person. Even Russia managed to reach nearly $11,000.

"Many think that Russia was a major economy. It is actually close to Spain in size, and way below those of China, India, Japan, Germany, the UK, France, and Italy. That was even before the sanctions hit Russia. True, it is important in some sectors, primarily energy, lumber, nickel, and uranium are examples.

"On a global scale, this level of national income per capita puts Ukraine lower than 150th in the world. Countries that are usually considered poor, such as Bolivia, Bangladesh, and Pakistan have significantly higher numbers. The most successful countries, such as Singapore, are almost 30 times higher than Ukraine was prior to the war."

"Why is that?"

"To understand why, we need to look at Ukraine's economic history before nationhood, as far back as the middle of the 19th Century. Divided between the Tsarist and the Austro-Hungarian empires, Ukraine was exploited. Both empires restricted freedom and development. Satisfying imperial needs for agricultural and industrial production were paramount. Later renewed Polish invasions caused further disruption."

"The eastern part of Ukraine, held by the Tsars, had the best agricultural land. That highly productive area was removed from international trade by the Russian Federation during the recent war.

"World War I turned Ukraine into a battleground once again. The Bolshevik Revolution allowed a brief hope for Ukrainian independence. The Soviets ruthlessly put these aspirations down.

"In the 1930s, Stalin's collective farming, genocide, ethnic cleansing, and exporting the people's food, destroyed the agricultural economy, starving millions. At the same time, the Soviets emphasized heavy industry in Kyiv, Mariupol, and other cities. Ethnic Russians were moved into the city centers to try and erase Ukrainian identity and language.

"In World War II, both the Russians and Germans added to the human suffering. The entire economy was wrecked."

"So how can you possibly be hopeful, now it has happened again?"

"Because there are levers that will be pulled to create success. This can be much greater than just a replacement of the lackluster situation of 2020.

"Permit me to elaborate, using lessons from other situations. One is the so called German Economic Miracle after 1945. It was no miracle at all. It was a series of factors which might well be replicated in Ukraine today.

"We've all seen the pictures, showing German cities in ruins. Berlin was like Kyiv, or worse. The people were living in abject poverty, without basic amenities. They were digging and removing the rubble by hand.

"At least five things sped German recovery.

"First, the occupying powers were there to keep order and organize essentials. Of course, in their zone, the reds were as busy raping and looting in the early stages. Then they removed all machinery they could to serve Soviet needs.

"Second, as is already happening in the Ukraine, aid was pouring in for reconstruction. Western governments provided not only food and essentials, but also grants and loans at favorable interest rates. Marshall Aid was the main example. Corporations like General Motors were subsidised to up plants in the then low wage Germany.

"In today's Ukraine, foreign aid, investment, and enterprises will enable a rapid change. It will fund reconstructing infrastructure and giving the people what they need to hasten recovery.

"Third, and this is a point many failed to see, the whole of Germany was not utterly destroyed. Let me use the example of a railway. The stations bridges and yards were bombed. By rebuilding these, the benefits of the whole line, including undamaged parts, became productive. In other words, if it took say $5 million to build a railroad, the damaged parts may only have cost $2.5 million to reconstruct. You then had a $5 million railroad for only half the investment. Much of the economy was like that. So it will be in Ukraine.

"A fourth factor in Germany was leapfrogging old technology. In any economy there is both old and modern machinery. Similarly, some people have obsolete skills. New training is needed for the future.

Ukraine Refugees

A good example is the way cell phones are changing poor economies around the world. They need not waste money putting up wires in remote areas. The people learn how to use the cell phones' computer power and access to the internet to trade and innovate in their jobs. Old machinery in the Ukraine can be replaced with the latest available, which is more productive.

"Much manufacturing and other investment will go to the Ukraine because labor costs are by far the lowest in Europe. The incentives will accelerate this.

"The last thing will be the reduced population. In Germany at the end of World War II, many were dead or imprisoned. In the Ukraine, there were about 44 million people. Perhaps most of the possibly 4 million external refugees will return. There may be future outflows as people experience higher standards of living in other countries. They will send remittances to relatives still in the country. These funds will boost further development.

"There may be 10 million displaced persons inside Ukraine. Many cannot return to their old homes and jobs. There is a new mobile and motivated labor force.

"A falling in population is analogous to the black death plagues across Europe. Before a third or more of a population was wiped out, the rulers could dominate the people. Owning the land was the important thing. The serfs were tied to it.

"When workers became scarce, rulers competed to hire them. The old ways had to go. New and more productive methods of using the land and of manufacturing were invented. People moved to where the opportunities were.

"So you can see why I am optimistic."

"You also draw lessons from the former German Democratic Republic, professor."

"Indeed, there we had a laboratory experiment across two competing economic systems. Neither was perfect, by the way. I will contrast them in a very crude way, simply to make the point. There were, and still are, many flaws in the economy of the Federal Republic. Back then, the way the families of ex-Nazis were allowed to reclaim their businesses was a sore point. It did provide continuity.

"In the GDR, the state owned pretty much everything. Plans were made centrally, some in Moscow for the whole Soviet Empire. Workers were paid according to set scales. The value of their output was less important than the Communist image. Position in the Party was more relevant than management capability. Corruption was rife. Prices were decided centrally, irrespective of supply and demand. This led to shortages, queues, and black markets.

"A well-known saying in the GDR was that, 'Stalin pretends to pay us and we pretend to work.' As a result, the standard of living in East Germany fell way below that of the West. Many fled west due to oppression and poor conditions on one side and better opportunities on the other.

"The Federal Republic of Germany's model was that markets set prices. It encouraged productive enterprise. The opportunity to do well rewarded innovation and initiative.

"The consequences of all this continued in the East, long after the fall of the Berlin Wall. The ingrained culture of needing to cheat the system, minimizing effort and lack of initiative, persisted amongst many. Productivity in the new eastern federal states of Germany is still way behind that of the western ones.

"In short, we can expect a difficult period for those returning to their homes in Ukraine. However, with determination and international support, they can be substantially better off than in the first place in the next ten to twenty years.

"Professor, please comment on President Biden's remark that Ukraine is the breadbasket of the world, and the Russian invasion contributed much to world inflation."

"It is not for me to comment on the statements of world leaders. I can say that disruptions from wars and sanctions impact the world's economies in many complicated ways.

"It is worth remarking on the world markets for grains. The Ukraine was a relatively small producer. For example, China produces around 133 million metric tons of wheat; India is next with 104 million. Of course, both these countries have so many mouths to feed that they import more than they produce. The US, at 52 million metric tons, and Canada, at 32 million, are major exporters. Ukraine only produced 28 million tons, but contributed to export markets. Corn, millet, and sunflower products all follow similar patterns."

"What of Russia's primary products?"

"Well, primary energy and transmission are hugely important in Europe. Sanctions on energy hit the Europeans as much as the Russians in the medium term. This is especially true for Germany. The US is self-sufficient. Other factors are the main causes of inflation in prices there. Sanctions on Iran and Venezuela also impact energy inflation, but so does the accelerated move to green energy.

Russia is the world's most important nickel producer and an important supplier of uranium. The US was wise enough not to sanction these products. Overall it would be surprising if sanctions on products were not scaled back very rapidly.

Ukraine Refugees

Many sanctions on individuals may remain, but may well be mainly cosmetic, to satisfy those blaming individuals for what happened. Some will be rolled back.

Author's Notes

I share these thoughts as a deeply flawed human being, who has made many mistakes in my life. I am lucky enough to have the time and to be in a situation to think about things other than the hourly struggle for survival, and against pain suffering and hardship, which many face.

This book had to be written quickly. Media and public interest and attention are fickle. Readers might remember when people posted that they were all "Charlie Hedbo." Global warming and pollution compete for headlines with people's immediate concerns. COVID news waxes and wanes.

For just over a month, Ukraine dominated media interest. That is already fading fast. The UK media was soon obsessing about the color of a Princess' dress on visiting those globally important ex-colonies in the Caribbean.

Inflation versus the pay of the masses, shortages of desired goods, gender and woke politics, political scandals, and local politics are elbowing Ukraine from the headlines. People who genuinely care about refugees are becoming aware that there are many times more of them in other parts of the world.

A disturbing trend is the capture of the media by the propagandists. It is possible to discover different points of view, but it became ever more difficult as the media oligarchs on all sides shut down opposing perspectives. The media presented statements and news from military and clandestine sources and from various political parties as facts. They still do. We live in an Orwellian world

The US has undoubtedly won the media war, and quite possibly the proxy war it has fought with the lives of Ukrainians.

In this book, I sought to give a balanced view.

Questions Readers Might Consider

If you are kind enough to read this book, without tossing it aside as not fitting your views of the world, you might want to ask yourself these questions:

1. What were my preferred and main sources of information about Ukraine?
2. Did I consider where the main sources of information came from?
3. How much were the opinions expressed by journalists and my contacts influenced by the military, the industries which benefitted from the conflict, and clandestine services, from which countries?
4. Did I seek alternative information and opinions?
5. What percentage of my social media interest and posts were focused on Ukraine a month ago, two weeks ago, and today?
6. What is the ranking of the matters of most concern to me personally today?
7. Are Ukrainian refugees more important to me than those from Africa, Asia, or Latin America?

8. If so, why is that?
9. If so, why is that?
10. Is Russia still a threat to world peace?
11. Can this be sustained, given the small size of the Russian economy?

About the Author

Aaron Aalborg is a nom de plume. Born into modest beginnings in the UK, he spent his first eleven years in social housing.

He benefited from the UK's then free education and has degrees in economics and business.

He was lucky in learning many things around the world from his work and studies. At various times he was: a trainee Catholic monk; a student radical; a green beret commando; a worker in the food, groceries, and construction businesses; a partner in a Chicago management consultancy; advisor to governments and corporations in many countries; an investment banker; the leader of a global executive search firm; a part time and a peripatetic business school professor; and teacher in the UK, Eastern Europe, Asia, Belgium and the Netherlands.

He and his Scottish wife have lived and worked in Europe, the US, Asia, and Latin America.

His many interests include geo-politics, history, philosophy, world religions, strategy, martial arts, ecology, and writing. Perhaps he is a jack of all trades and master of none.

He spends his time between, Latin America, North America, and Europe.

His enjoyment in writing is largely motivated by supplying provocative ideas and information to readers.

Other Books by the Author

Written as Aaron Aalborg

They Deserved It - Both a historical and contemporary novel, it is based on a true story about women poisoning their husbands in 17thCentury Italy. It is a fast-moving thriller. There is a cast of abused young women, rascally husbands, witches, evil cardinals, and a horrible Pope. The discovery of a mysterious Egyptian box moves the story into contemporary New York. There, a rogue lawyer and her lesbian lover, the head of an IT company, continue the murders. There is a thrilling pursuit around the world, before the unexpected finale.

Revolution - A thrilling account of the assassination of multiple heads of state, including the U.S. President and the British royal family. It is set in the near future. A socialist revolution and world-wide mayhem follow. The U.S. and the world descend into chaos. There is furious action and a dramatic terminal twist.

Doom, Gloom and Despair - A collection of short stories set in different countries, including the US, France, Costa Rica and others. They include dramas around failed rebellions, packs of ravenous dogs, volcanic eruptions, duelling deities and a suicide cult. These sardonically dark stories feature man-eating animals, cannibals, and other bleak events. Perfect for potential suicides and those of sensitive disposition, or perhaps not.

Cooking the Rich, A Post-Revolutionary Necessity - This spoof cookbook includes hilarious recipes for cooking Donald Trump, The British Royal Family, billionaires, and Middle Eastern potentates. The author still wonders why he is still alive.

Terminated - The Making of a Serial Killer - volume one - from the slums to the Falklands War - In this thriller Alex, a poor boy from Scotland and a martial artist, beats the odds to win a top education. He becomes a successful businessman. Recruited by a crack special services unit, he is embroiled in the Falklands War with Argentina. He returns an unsung hero. There is non-stop excitement. His personal life is equally dramatic.

Terminated - The Making of a Serial Killer - volume two - from hero to serial killer - Alex returns to a stellar international business career. He soon becomes embroiled in the evils of the business world. He meets psychopaths in politics, through top management consulting, and in investment banking. After murders and assassinations, he becomes CEO of an executive search firm. He discovers that headhunting is as corrupt as everything else. After trying to fight his demons in a Buddhist monastery, he returns like an avenging angel to eliminate those he feels deserve it.

Save the Bonsai - An unusual novel, part Sci-Fi, part fantasy and part cataclysmic thriller; it breaks the rules of all these genres - A Transgender Japanese breeds killer plants. They spread around the world. Much of the action is in Japan and the US. The book has sardonic humor. It reflects today's problems of greed, lust for power and just lust, playing on human gullibility.

Coming in 2022

Tales of a Misspent Life - This is the working title for a series of entertaining, scandalous, and hilarious true stories and anecdotes from the authors experiences in over a hundred countries.

Written as Chris J Clarke

Blood-Axe: The Saga of a 21st Century Viking - Many readers are fascinated by tales about the Vikings. They allow us to escape into an exciting bygone era, unencumbered by the inconvenient restrictions of tedious civilization.

Blood-Axe is a modern fantasy tale of men and women who form a Viking re-enactment group. Carried away, they destroy an English town amidst witchcraft, blood sacrifice, slaughter, rape and pillage.

It is a rollicking mix of hilariously crazy scenes; scary social comment on the inner Viking within all of us and a cliff hanging thriller with a most unusual plot.

Printed in Great Britain
by Amazon